Picture Book Studio USA

Lark Carrier THERE WAS A HILL...

Copyright © 1985 Lark Carrier
Published in USA by Picture Book Studio USA,
an imprint of Neugebauer Press USA Inc.
Distributed by Alphabet Press, Natick, MA.
Distributed in Canada by Vanwell Publishing, St. Catharines, Ont.
Published in U.K. by Neugebauer Press Publishing Ltd., London.
Distributed by A & C Black PLC, London.
Distributed in Australia by Hutchinson Group Australia Pty Ltd.
Printed in Austria.

LIBRARY OF CONGRESS CATALOGING IN PUBLICATION DATA

Carrier, Lark, 1947–
There was a hill.

Summary: Hills, trunks, leaves, and other objects
are transformed into bears, elephants, moths,
and other things as the reader turns the page.
1. Children's stories. 2. Toy and movable
books – Specimens. [1. Toy and movable books]
I. Title.
PZ7.C23453Th   1984   [E]   84-25536
ISBN O-9O7234-7O-4

Lark Carrier THERE WAS A HILL...

There was a hill

that climbed a tree

that hauled a stump

that chased a stick

that bit a leaf

that hugged a limb

that scratched a rock

that laid an egg

that lit the hill that was...